Richard Hovey

Along the trail

A Book of Lyrics

Richard Hovey

Along the trail
A Book of Lyrics

ISBN/EAN: 9783744771986

Printed in Europe, USA, Canada, Australia, Japan

Cover: Foto ©Andreas Hilbeck / pixelio.de

More available books at **www.hansebooks.com**

ALONG THE TRAIL

A BOOK OF LYRICS
BY RICHARD HOVEY

SCIRE

QVOD · SCIENDVM

BOSTON
SMALL, MAYNARD
AND COMPANY
1899

BY SMALL, MAYNARD AND COMPANY

First Edition, December, 1898
Second Edition, March, 1899

THE UNIVERSITY PRESS, CAMBRIDGE, U.S.A.

TO MY MOTHER

The thanks of the author and the publishers are due to Messrs. Copeland and Day for their kind permission to use such extracts from Songs from Vagabondia and More Songs from Vagabondia as were necessary in order to print "Comrades," "Spring," and "The Faun" in this volume with their complete text.

CONTENTS

I

II

III

IV

V

ALONG THE TRAIL

1883–1898

I

THE WORD OF THE LORD FROM HAVANA

THUS spake the Lord:
Because ye have not heard,
Because ye have given no heed
To my people in their need;

Because the oppressed cried
From the dust where he died,
And ye turned your face away
From his cry in that day,

Because ye have bought and sold
That which is above gold,
Because your brother is slain
While ye get you drunk with gain,

(Behold, these are my people, I have brought them to
    birth,
On whom the mighty have trod,
The kings of the earth,
Saith the Lord God!)

Because ye have fawned and bowed down
Lest the spoiler frown,
And the wrongs that the spoiled have borne
Ye have held in scorn,

Therefore with rending and flame
I have marred and smitten you,

3

Therefore I have given you to shame,
That the nations shall spit on you.

Therefore my Angel of Death
Hath stretched out his hand on you,
Therefore I speak in my wrath,
Laying command on you;

(Once have I bared my sword,
And the kings of the earth gave a cry;
Twice have I bared my sword,
That the kings of the earth should die;
Thrice shall I bare my sword,
And ye shall know my name, that it is I!)

Ye who held peace less than right
When a king laid a pitiful tax on you,
Hold not your hand from the fight
When freedom cries under the axe on you!

(I who called France to you, call you to Cuba in turn!
Repay — lest I cast you adrift and you perish astern!)

Ye who made war that your ships
Should lay to at the beck of no nation,
Make war now on Murder, that slips
The leash of her hounds of damnation!

Ye who remembered the Alamo,
Remember the Maine!

Ye who unfettered the slave,
Break a free people's chain !

(*Written after the* **destruction of the battleship** *"Maine,"*
17 *February,* 1898)

THE CALL OF THE BUGLES

BUGLES !
And the Great Nation thrills and leaps to arms !
Prompt, unconstrained, immediate,
Without misgiving and without debate,
Too calm, too strong for fury or alarms,
The people blossoms armies and puts forth
The splendid summer of its noiseless might;
For the old sap **of** fight
Mounts up in South and North,
The thrill
That tingled in our veins at Bunker **Hill**
And brought to bloom July of 'Seventy-Six !
Pine and palmetto mix
With the sequoia of the giant West
Their ready banners, and the hosts of war,
Near and far,
Sudden as dawn,
Innumerable as forests, hear the call
Of the bugles,
The battle-birds !

For not alone the brave, the fortunate,
Who first of all
Have put their knapsacks on —
They are the valiant vanguard of the rest! —
Not they alone, but all our millions wait,
Hand on sword,
For the word
That bids them bid the nations know us sons of Fate.

Bugles!
And in my heart a cry,
— Like a dim echo far and mournfully
Blown back to answer them from yesterday!
A soldier's burial!
November hillsides and the falling leaves
Where the Potomac broadens to the tide —
The crisp autumnal silence and the gray
(As of a solemn ritual
Whose congregation glories as it grieves,
Widowed but still a bride) —
The long hills sloping to the wave,
And the lone bugler standing by the grave!

Taps!
The lonely call over the lonely woodlands —
Rising like the soaring of wings,
Like the flight of an eagle —
Taps!
They sound forever in my heart.

From farther still,
The echoes — still the **echoes** !
The bugles of the dead
Blowing **from** spectral ranks an answering cry !
The ghostly roll of immaterial drums,
Beating reveille in the camps of dream,
As from far meadows comes,
Over the pathless hill,
The irremeable stream.
I hear the tread
Of the great armies of the Past go by ;
I hear,
Across the **wide sea** wash of years between,
Concord and Valley Forge shout back from the unseen,
And Vicksburg **give a cheer.**

Our cheer goes back to them, the valiant dead !
Laurels and roses on their graves to-day,
Lilies and laurels over them we lay,
And violets o'er each unforgotten head.
Their honor still with the returning May
Puts on its springtime in our memories,
Nor till the last American with them lies
Shall the young year forget to strew their bed.

Peace to their ashes, sleep and honored rest !
But we — awake !
Ours to remember them with deeds like theirs !

From sea to sea the insistent bugle blares,
The drums will not be still for any sake ;
And as an eagle rears his crest,
Defiant, from some tall pine of the north,
And spreads his wings to fly,
The banners of America go forth
Against the clarion sky.
Veteran and volunteer,
They who were comrades of that shadow host,
And the young brood whose veins renew the fires
That burned in their great sires,
Alike we hear
The summons sounding clear
From coast to coast, —
The cry of the bugles,
The battle-birds !

As some great hero men have dreamed might be,
Sigurd or Herakles or Launcelot,
Too strong to reckon up the gain or pain,
With equal and indifferent disdain
Keeping or keeping not
What he may win,
Gives to the world his victory
And to the weak the labors he might spare,
My knightly country, the world's paladin,
Throw out its pennon to the air
To make a people free !

Rejoice, O Cuba! thy worst foe
Is overthrown.
The money dragon,
The Old **Serpent,**
Thy jailer's strong **defence, laid low,**
Cast down,
Pierced to **the** bone,
Makes off to nurse his wound,
Dragging his scaly length along the ground.
Ha, ha! he is sick,
He hath no stomach for the battle.
With dull reptilian malice in his eyes,
Spoiled of his prey, he lies,
Blinking his glutton hatred from his lair.
Plotting new outrage **in** his den,
He waits to be strong again.
— Let him beware!
For we, who have smitten him once,
Shall smite him again!
A passing wound for the nonce,
But a death blow then!
Now with a warning stroke,
That he coil not across our way
When the wronged cry under the yoke
And we may not stay;
But then in the hour of Doom
To his irrevocable tomb
Forever hurled,

9

That the world may again have room
For the sons of the world.

Rejoice again, O Cuba!
Rejoice, Gomez!
Rejoice, spirit of Maceo!
The voice of the Lord in the drums,
The cry of Jehovah in the bugles;
— Let my people go free!
Behold, I will burst their chain!
For my Deliverer comes,
He whom I have chosen to be
My Messenger on the Sea,
My Rod for the scourge of Spain!
I have endured her too long;
I have smitten and she has not ceased from wrong, —
I have forborne
And she has held me in scorn.
Now therefore for her misdeeds
Wherewith Time bleeds,
I who smote her by the hand of Drake
And wrenched from her the Sea, —
I who raised up Bolivar to shake
Her captive continent free, —
I will smite her for the third time in my wrath
And naught shall remain,
But a black char of memory in man's path,
Of the power of Spain.

We have heard the voice of the Lord;
Manila knows our answer, and Madrid
Shall hear it in our cannon at her gate,
Unless to save some remnant of her fate,
Ere that assault be bid,
She yield her conquered sword.

Let her not put her trust
In the nations that cry out
Against us, in them that flout
The battle of the just.
They have made themselves drunk with wind;
They have uttered a foolish cry
In the ears of the Lord on high;
But they shall not save her with words
— Nay, nor with swords —
From the doom of the sin she has sinned.

For the writ of the Powers does not run
Where the flag of the Union floats.
Fair and equal every one
We greet with loyal throats;
But we own no suzerain.
Thewed with freedom,
Mailed in destiny —
We shall maintain
Against the world our right,
Their peer in majesty, their peer in might.

Who now are they whose God is gain?
Let Rothschild-ridden Europe hold her peace!
Her jest is proved a lie.
They and not we refrain
From all things high
At the money-changers' cry;
They and not we have sold
Their flags for gold;
They and not we yield honor to increase.

Honor to England, that she does us right
At last, and, after many a valiant fight,
Forgets her ancient grudge!
But ye, O nations, be the Lord our judge
And yours the shame forever! How shall ye
In the unforgetting face of History
Look without blush hereafter? Ye who gave
To the Great Robber all your words of cheer,
And to the Champion of the Right a sneer—
What answer will ye have
When affronted Time demands
The shame and fame of nations at your hands?

Thou too, O France!
Thou, the beloved!—
Paul Jones and Lafayette in Paradise
Lift not their sad, ashamed, bewildered eyes,
But pass in silence with averted glance.

Twinned with us in the hearts of all the free,
O fair and dear, what have we done to thee?
What have we done to thee, beloved and fair,
That thou shouldst greet us with an alien stare,
And take to thy embrace
Her whose flag never flew but where it left the trace
Of murder and of rapine on the air?

Not only to lay low
The decrepit foe
— Proud, cruel, treacherous, but still brave,
With one foot in the grave —
But once for all
To warn the world that, though we do not brawl,
Our sword is ready to protect
The weak against the brutal strong,
Our guns are ready to exact
Justice of them that do us wrong.

Ay, we "remember the Maine,"
The mighty ship
And the men thereon!
There is no court for nations that can mete
The just reward for murder upon Spain;
No Arbiter can put the black cap on;
No sovereign nation, shorn of sovereignship,
Be brought, a felon, to the judgment seat
— Except by war!

Cease then this silly prate,
That to do justice on the evil-doer
Is vengeful and unworthy of the State.
Remember the Maine —
That all the world as well as Spain
May know that God has given us the sword
To punish crime and vindicate his word.
Ye pompous prattlers, cease
Your idle platitudes of peace
When there is no peace !
Back to your world of books, and leave the world of
    men
To them that have the habit of the real,
Nor longer with a mask of fair ideal
Hide your indifference to the facts of pain !

Not against war,
But against wrong,
League we in mighty bonds from sea to sea !
Peace, when the world is free !
Peace, when there is no thong,
Fetter nor bar !
No scourges for men's backs,
No thumbscrews and no racks —
For body or soul !
No unjust law !
No tyrannous control
Of brawn or maw !

But, though the day be far,
Till then, war !

Blow, bugles !
Over the rumbling drum and marching feet
Sound your high, sweet defiance to the air !
Great is war — great and fair !
The terrors of his face are grand and sweet,
And to the wise the calm of God is there.
God clothes himself in darkness as in light,
— The God of love, but still the God of might.
Nor love they least
Who strike with right good will
To vanquish ill
And fight God's battle upward from the beast.

By strife as well as loving — strife,
The Law of Life, —
In brute and man the climbing has been done
And shall be done hereafter.   Since man was,
No upward-climbing cause
Without the sword has ever yet been won.

Bugles !
The imperious bugles !
Still their call
Soars like an exaltation to the sky.
They call on men to fall,
To die, —

Remembered or forgotten, but a part
Of the great beating of the Nation's heart!
A call to sacrifice!
A call to victory!
Hark, in the Empyrean
The battle-birds!
The bugles!

(*Waldron Post*, *G. A. R.*, *Nyack*, *N. Y.*, *Memorial Day*
1898)

UNMANIFEST DESTINY

To what new fates, my country, far
   And unforeseen of foe or friend,
Beneath what unexpected star,
   Compelled to what unchosen end,

Across the sea that knows no beach
   The Admiral of Nations guides
Thy blind obedient keels to reach
   The harbor where thy future rides!

The guns that spoke at Lexington
   Knew not that God was planning then
The trumpet word of Jefferson
   To bugle forth the rights of men.

To them that wept and cursed Bull Run,
   What was it but despair and shame?

16

Who saw behind the cloud the sun?
  Who knew that God was in the flame?

Had not defeat upon defeat,
  Disaster on disaster come,
The slave's emancipated feet
  Had never marched behind the drum.

There is a Hand that bends our deeds
  To mightier issues than we planned,
Each son that triumphs, each that bleeds,
  My country, serves Its dark command.

I do not know beneath what sky
  Nor on what seas shall be thy fate;
I only know it shall be high,
  I only know it shall be great.

July, 1898

AMERICA

WE came to birth in battle; when we pass,
It shall be to the thunder of the drums.
We are not one that weeps and saith *Alas*,
Nor one that dreams of dim millenniums.
Our hand is set to this world's business,
And it must be accomplished workmanly;
Be we not stout enough to keep our place,
What profits it the world that we be free?

Not with despite for others, but to hold
Our station in the world inviolate,
We keep the stomach of the men of old
Who built in blood the bastions of our fate.
    We know not to what goal God's purpose tends;
    We know He works through battle to His ends.

October, 1898

DEAD

Aн God ! how strange the rattling in the street
    Comes to me where I lie and the hours pass.
I watch a beetle crawling up the sheet
That covers me, and curiously note
    The green and yellow back like mouldy brass,
And cannot even shudder at the thought
    How soon the loathsome thing will reach my face.

And by such things alone I measure out
    The slow drip of the minutes from Time's eaves.
For if I think of when I lived, I doubt
It was but yesterday I brushed the flowers;
    But when I think of what I am, thought leaves
The weak mind dizzy in a waste of hours.
    O God, how happy is the man that grieves !

Life ? It was life to look upon her face,
    And it was life to rage when she was gone ;
But this new horror !— In the market-place
A form, in all things like me as I moved
    Of old, is marked or hailed of many an one
That takes it for his friend that lived and loved, --
    And I laugh voicelessly, a laugh of stone.

For here I lie and neither move nor feel,
    And watch that Other pacing up and down
The room, or pausing at his potter's wheel

To turn out cunning vessels from the clay,
    Vessels that he will hawk about the town,
And then return to work another day
    Frowning; but I, — I neither smile nor frown.

I see him take his coat down from the peg
    And put it on, and open the white door,
And brush some bit of cobweb from his leg,
And look about the room before he goes;
    And then the clock goes ticking as before,
And I am with him and know all he does,
    And I am here and tell each clock-tick o'er.

And men are praising him for subtle skill;
    And women love him — God alone knows why!
He can have all the world holds at his will —
But this, to be a living soul, and this
    No man but I can give him; and I lie
And make no sign, and care not what he is,
    And hardly know if this indeed be I.

Ah, if she came and bent above me here,
    Who lie with straight bands bound about my
        chin!
Ah, if she came and stood beside this bier
With aureoles as of old upon her hair
    To light the darkness of this burial bin!
Should I not rise again and breathe the air
    And feel the veins warm that the blood beats in?

Or should I lie with sinews fixed and shriek
    As dead men shriek and make no sound? Should I
See her gray eyes look love and hear her speak,
And be all impotent to burst my shroud?
    Will the dead never rise from where they lie?
Or will they never cease to think so loud?
    Or is to know and not to be, to die?

1890

FORGIVEN

" DESPISE me if you will.   I have done you wrong, —
    Most grievous wrong, — but not the wrong you
    think.
You deemed me strongest where I was not strong,
    And martyr where a scratch would make me shrink.
Nor, false for truth's sake though I wrest my role,
    Am I one half so false as I am true ;
And mine own truth has throttled my proud soul
    And cast it prostrate at the feet of you.
I am most humble ; but my heart cries out
    For one last grace from you before we part ;
— Though it give pain, to hear my tale throughout
    And — not forgive — but understand my heart.
Therefore I bare my soul to you and tell
    The utter truth, though speaking so I seem
But a reiterate anguish to compel,
    That in condemning you may not condemn

You know not what, but me, me, me!" — The whole
  I told then, act and impulse; I kept not
Aught back that might reveal me to her soul:
  And she forgave, — but understood no jot.

   1893

LOVE AND CHANGE

One Lover

FOREVER? Ah, too vain to hope, my sweet,
  That love should linger when all else must die!
  No prayer can stay his wings, if he will fly,
  Nor longing lure him back to find our feet,
Weeping for old disloyalties. The heat
  That glows in the uplifting of thine eye,
  Dims and grows cold ere yet the day pass by;
  Nor ever will the dusk of love repeat
The dawn's pearl-rapture. Ay, it is the doom
  Of love that it must watch its own decay.
  Petal by petal from the voluptuous bloom
Drops withering, till the last is blown away.
  The night mists rise and shroud the bier of day,
  And we are left lamenting in the gloom.

Another Lover

"Love is eternal," sang I long ago
  Of some light love that lasted for a day;
  But when that whim of hearts was puffed away,
  And other loves that following made as though

24

They were the very deathless, lost the glow
   Youth mimics the divine with, and grew gray,
   I said, " It is a dream, — no love will stay."
   Angels have taught me wisdom ; now I know,
Though lesser loves, and greater loves, may cease,
   Love still endures, knocking at myriad gates
   Of beauty, — dawns and call of woodland birds,
Stars, winds, and waters, lilt of luted words
   And worshipped women, — till it finds its peace
   In the abyss where Godhead loves and waits.

A Third Lover

My love for you dies many times a year,
   And a new love is monarch in his place.
   Love must grow weary of the fairest face ;
   The fondest heart must fail to hold him near.
For love is born of wonder, kin to fear —
   Things grown familiar lose the sweet amaze ;
   Grown to their measure, love must turn his gaze
   To some new splendor, some diviner sphere.
But in the blue night of your endless soul
   New stars globe ever as the old are scanned ;
   Goal where love will, you reach a farther goal,
And the new love is ever love of you.
   Love needs a thousand loves, forever new,
   And finds them — in the hollow of your hand.

   1897

LAUNCELOT AND GAWAINE

Two women loved a poet. One was dark,
Luxuriant with the beauty of the south,
A heart of fire — and this one he forsook.
The other slender, tall, with wide gray eyes,
Who loved him with a still intensity
That made her heart a shrine — to her he clave,
And he was faithful to her to the end.
And when the poet died, a song was found
Which he had writ, of Launcelot and Gawaine;
And when the women read it, one cried out:
" Where got he Launcelot? Gawaine I know —
He drew that picture from a looking-glass —
Sleek, lying, treacherous, golden-tongued Gawaine ! "
The other, smiling, murmured " Launcelot ! "

1888

MY LADY'S SOUL

LIKE some enchanted dweller in the deep,
I swim among the grottoes of your soul.
Far, far away the cliffs rise rough and steep;
Far, far above the ruffling billows roll.
Here a new world, unseen of any eye
But mine, unfolds its unfamiliar blooms
In opal calms unuttered to the sky
And tremulous light of phosphorescent glooms.

And if my soul revisit the raw day,
For joy of all that secret beauty blind,
I, merman-like, have little care to stay
In the thin air, but plunge again to find
Those deeps unvisited from which I came,
Whose simplest wonders have not yet a name.

1895

AFTER BUSINESS HOURS

WHEN I sit down with thee at last alone,
Shut out the wrangle of the clashing day,
The scrape of petty jars that fret and fray,
The snarl and yelp of brute beasts for a bone;
When thou and I sit down at last alone,
And through the dusk of rooms divinely gray
Spirit to spirit finds its voiceless way,
As tone melts meeting in accordant tone, —
Oh, then our souls, far in the vast of sky,
Look from a tower, too high for sound of strife
Or any violation of the town,
Where the great vacant winds of God go by,
And over the huge misshapen city of life
Love pours his silence and his moonlight down.

1898

THE THOUGHT OF HER

My love for thee doth take me unaware,
    When most with lesser things my brain is wrought,
    As in some nimble interchange of thought
    The silence enters, and the talkers stare.
Suddenly I am still and thou art there,
    A viewless visitant and unbesought,
    And all my thinking trembles into nought
    And all my being opens like a prayer.
Thou art the lifted Chalice in my soul,
    And I a dim church at the thought of thee;
    Brief be the moment, but the mass is said,
The benediction like an aureole
    Is on my spirit, and shuddering through me
    A rapture like the rapture of the dead.

1898

LOVE IN THE WINDS

When I am standing on a mountain crest,
Or hold the tiller in the dashing spray,
My love of you leaps foaming in my breast,
Shouts with the winds and sweeps to their foray;
My heart bounds with the horses of the sea,
And plunges in the wild ride of the night,
Flaunts in the teeth of tempest the large glee
That rides out Fate and welcomes gods to fight.
Ho, love, I laugh aloud for love of you,

Glad that our love is fellow to rough weather, —
No fretful orchid hothoused from the dew,
But hale and hardy as the highland heather,
    Rejoicing in the wind that stings and thrills,
    Comrade of ocean, playmate of the hills.

1898

TWO AND FATE

THE ship we ride the world in sniffs the storm,
And throws its head up to the hurricane,
Quivering like a war-horse when ranks form
With scream of bugles and the shout of men,
Neighs to the challenge of the thunderbolt,
And charges in the squadrons of the surge,
Sabring its way with fury of revolt
And lashed with exaltation as a scourge!
Who would not rather founder in the fight
Than not have known the glory of the fray?
Ay, to go down in armor and in might,
With our last breath to dominate dismay,
    To sink amid the mad sea's clashing spears
    And with the cry of bugles in our ears!

1898

FAITH AND FATE

To horse, my dear, and out into the night!
Stirrup and saddle and away, away!
Into the darkness, into the affright,

Into the unknown on our trackless way!
Past bridge and town missiled with flying feet,
Into the wilderness our riding thrills;
The gallop echoes through the startled street,
And shrieks like laughter in the demoned hills;
Things come to meet us with fantastic frown,
And hurry past with maniac despair;
Death from the stars looks ominously down —
Ho, ho, the dauntless riding that we dare!
    East, to the dawn, or west or south or north!
    Loose rein upon the neck of Fate — and forth!

1898

CHANSONS DE ROSEMONDE

I

THE dawn is lonely for the sun,
    And chill and drear;
The one lone star is pale and wan
    As one in fear.
But when day strides across the hills,
    The warm blood rushes through
    The bared soft bosom of the blue
And all the glad east thrills.

Oh, come, my King!   The hounds of joy
    Are waiting for thy horn

To chase the doe of heart's desire
    Across the heights of morn.
Oh, come, my Sun, and let me know
    The rapture of the day!
Oh, come, my love! Oh, come, my love!
    Thou art so long away!

II

Love, hold me close to thee —
    And kiss me — so —
Dear! . . . The green leaves above
    Blur in the blue;
The ground reels like a sea! . . .
    I know, I know
There is but now for love
    Between us two.

        .

Death like a wizard holds
    Me with his eye;
I cannot strive nor start,
    To break the spell! . . .
Night smothers in her folds
    My passing cry! . . .
But hold me to thy heart
    And all is well.

Ah, what if heaven should be
    A dream like this,
— Too glad to move,
    Too still to laugh or weep,
So thou stand over me,
    Bend down and kiss
My lips once — love —
    And let me fall asleep !

1894

A WANDERER

(Reminiscence of an old Scotch song)

EAST and west and north and south
I range o'er land and sea;
And I bear dead kisses on my mouth,
And dead love wearies me.
    I am caught up as a feather
    That the winds toss to and fro.
    Since we dwell not together,
    What care I where I go?

North and south and east and west
I drift on alien tides;
The one place where I may not rest
Is that where she abides.

So on through wind and weather!
Afar o'er land and sea!
If we be not together
What matter where we be?

1890

THE LOVE OF A BOY — YESTERDAY

No lips nor lutes can let thee know
The joy that lightens through my woe, —
But look in thine own heart, and so
I shall not need to tell thee, love.
 Lady of the winsome smile!
 Lovesome lady! Gentle lady!
 If my heart had any guile,
 Thou wouldst make me truthful, love.

Though bitter be our luckless lot,
It were more sad if love were not —
And all the rest may be forgot,
But thou wilt not forget me, love —
 Lady of the faithful heart!
 Loving lady! Loyal lady!
 Were I noble as thou art,
 No king's sword need knight me, love.

Were I myself a mighty king
With thousands at my beckoning,

3   33

My power were but a little thing
To do thee worthy honor, love.
        Lady in whose life I live!
        Fearless lady!   Peerless lady!
        If the stars were mine to give
        They should be thy necklace, love.

1889

✝ THE LOVE OF A BOY — TO-DAY

HEIGH-HO ! my thoughts are far away;
For wine or books I have no care;
I like to think upon the way
She has of looking very fair.
        Oh, work is nought, and play is nought,
        And all the livelong day is nought;
        There 's nothing much I care to learn
        But what her lovely lips have taught.

The campus cannot tempt me out,
The classics cannot keep me in ;
The only place I care about
Is where perchance she may have been.
        Oh, work is nought, and play is nought,
        And all the livelong day is nought;
        There 's nothing much I care to find
        Except the way she would be sought.

The train across the valley screams,
And like a hawk sweeps out of sight;
It bears me to her in my dreams
By day and night, by day and night.
　　Oh, work is nought, and play is nought,
　　And all the livelong day is nought;
　　There 's nothing much I care to be,
　　If I be only in her thought.

1897

AN OFF-SHORE VILLANELLE

OVER the dun depths where the white shark swims,
Waiting his fated prey with hungry eyes,
Swiftly the light skiff skims.

The laughing skipper trims
Seaward his course. What recks he that it lies
Over the dun depths where the white shark swims?

He shouts for glee in the mad wind's teeth. Fast dims
The land to a low long cloud-line in the skies.
Swiftly the light skiff skims,

Brushing the foaming brims
Of the wave-beakers as in mirth it flies
Over the dun depths where the white shark swims.

What brings the white girl there, about whose limbs
The wet skirts cling, as stormward, petrel-wise,
Swiftly the light skiff skims?

The strong sea-devils wreak their cruel whims
In vain.   Who heeds the hatred of their cries?
Swiftly the light skiff skims
Over the dun depths where the white shark swims.

1888

TO LESBIA

(From the Latin of Catullus)

LIVE we, Lesbia, and love !
What though the greybeards disapprove !
Let them wag their toothless jaws !
Who cares a copper for their saws?

Suns may set and suns may rise,
But when the light of life once dies,
Night that knows not any dawn
Brings eternal slumber on.

Kisses, kisses, I implore —
A hundred more ! a thousand more !
Another thousand — ah, too fleet ! —
A hundred ! — thousand ! — hundred, sweet !

Let the thousands throng and cumber !
Crush them, crowd them past all number,
Lest some enchanter blight our blisses,
Knowing the number of our kisses.

1888

NOCTURNE

WHITE, white I remember her —
  White from her forehead to her feet.
The moonlight falling through the pane
  Was not so white, was not so sweet.

She was a pool of moonlight there
  Between the window and the wall,
And the slow minutes bathed in her
  And went away beyond recall.

1898

✝ ## THE TWO LOVERS

THE lover of her body said:
  " She is more beautiful than night, —
But like the kisses of the dead
  Is my despair, and my delight."

The lover of her soul replied:
  "She is more wonderful than death, —
But bitter as the aching tide
  Is all the speech of love she saith."

The lover of her body said:
  " To know one secret of her heart,
For all the joy that I have had,
  Is past the reach of all my art."

37

The lover of her soul replied:
  " The secrets of her heart are mine, —
Save how she lives, a riven bride,
  Between the dust and the divine."

The lover of her body sware:
  " Though she should hate me, wit you well,
Rather than yield one kiss of her
  I give my soul to burn in hell."

The lover of her soul cried out:
  " Rather than leave her to your greed,
I would that I were walled about
  With death, — and death were death indeed ! "

The lover of her body wept,
  And got no good of all his gain,
Knowing that in her heart she kept
  The penance of the other's pain.

The lover of her soul went mad,
  But when he did himself to death,
Despite of all the woe he had,
  He smiled as one who vanquisheth.

  1898

APPARITION

(*From the* French of Mallarmé)

THE moon grew sad in heaven. In tears the seraphim,
A-dream with bow in fingers, in the calm of dim

Mists of unbodied flowers, from dying viols drew
The glide of white sobs over the corollas blue
— It was the day thy first kiss hallowed and made dumb.
My musing that delights to bring me martyrdom,
Grew wisely drunken with that sad scent of things reft
That, though without regret or aftertaste, is left,
Culling a dream, in him whose heart has culled the
    dream.
So strayed I on, with eyes on the worn walk a-gleam,
Where in the street and in the evening, out o' the air
Thou cam'st to me, all laughters, sunlight in thy hair.
And I believed I saw the fay with hat of gold
Who o'er spoiled childhood's slumber beautiful, of old
Passed, letting ever from her loosely closing hands
White clusters snow of stars, with odors of far lands.

  1895

SUMMER SADNESS

(From the French of Mallarmé)

THE sunlight on the sands, fair struggler fallen asleep,
  Makes warm a bath of languors in your golden hair,
And, burning away the angry incense that you weep,
  Mingles a wanton drink of longings in the air.

Immutable in calm, the white flamboyant day
  Has made you sigh (alas, my kisses full of qualms!)
" No, we shall never be one mummy, swathed for aye
  Under the ancient desert and the happy palms."

This incubus of soul we suffer, in the river
Of your warm hair might plunge and drown without a
    shiver,
And find that Nothingness that you know nothing of.
  And I would taste those tears of rouge beneath
    your eyes,
To see if they can give the heart you smote with love
  The insensibility of stones and summer skies.

1895

SONNET

(From the French of Mallarmé)

SPRUNG from the vase's bulge and leap
  Of fragile glass, the neck in gloom
  Fades out nor decks with any bloom
The bitter vigil that I keep.

Oh, I am sure that no lips e'er
  (Nay not her lover's nor my mother's)
  Have drunk the same dream as another's,
I,—sylph of the cold ceiling there!

The virgin chalice of no wine
  But an exhaustless widowhood,—
  It suffers, but is not subdued
(Oh, kiss naïve and saturnine!)
  To breathe forth aught that might disclose
  Within the shadows any rose.

  1895

40

SONNET

(*From the French of Mallarmé*)

BALMY with years, what silken ply,
    Whereo'er the fancy pines and pales,
    Is worth the tangled native veils
That in your mirror I descry?

Uplifted in the avenue,
    The tattered banners droop and dream;
    For me your naked tresses stream,
To drown my eyes in, glad of you.

No, never will the **lips be sure**
    Of any taste in **aught** they take
    Unless your princely lover **make,**
Amid that clustered cynosure,
    Die, as a diamond might die,
    The Glories and their smothered cry.

    1895

HERODIAS

(**From** *the French of Mallarmé*)

HERODIAS

AY, for myself, myself I flower forlorn!
You amethystine gardens buried deep
In wise abysses dim and bottomless,
You understand ; and you, neglected gold,

Keeping your ancient glory unprofaned
Under the dark sleep of primeval earth;
You, stones wherefrom mine eyes, like limpid gems,
Borrow their blaze melodious; and you,
Metals that give the tresses of my youth
A deadly splendor in their massive fall!

As for thee, woman born in centuries
Malign for the iniquities that lurk
In caverns Sibylline, — thou who darest to speak
Of one for whom, a mortal, shall from the cup
Of my slipped robes, aroma savage-sweet,
Rise the white shudder of my nakedness, —
Foretell that if the warm blue summer sky
That woman natively unveils before,
See me in my star-shivering shamefastness,
I die!

      The horror of virginity
Delights me; I would live, amid the fright
The touch of mine own hair can make me know,
To feel, at eve, within my couch withdrawn,
Inviolate reptile, in the useless flesh
Cold scintillation of thy pallid light,
Thou dying, thou consumed with chastity,
White night of icicles and cruel snow!

And thy lone sister, O my sister aye,
My dream shall rise to thee; even now so clear,

So wondrous clear the heart that dreamed it so,
I seem alone in my lone native land,
With all about me in **idolatry,**
Before a glass whose sleeping calm reflects
Herodias, with clear look of diamond . . .
Oh, last charm . . . yes . . . I **feel** it, I am alone.

NURSE

You will die, **lady?**

HERODIAS

        No, good grandam, **no.**
Be calm and leave **me;** pardon this **hard** heart.
First close the shutters, if you will.   The **sky**
Smiles like a seraph in the pane's profound,
And I detest the beautiful **sky.**

            The waves
Cradle themselves, and, yonder, know you not
A country where the inauspicious heaven
Shows Venus' hated aspects, **who** to-night
Burns in the leafage? Thither will **I go.**
Light again — call it child's play if you will —
Those tapers where the wax at the light flame
Weeps in the idle gold an alien tear,
And. . . .

NURSE

    Now?

HERODIAS
    Farewell.   [*Exit Nurse.*

43

                              You lie, O naked flower
Of my lips!
                    I await a thing unknown!
Heedless, perhaps, of the mystery and your cries,
Though you fling out the supreme murdered sobs
Of maidenhood that feels amid its dreams
Its chill gems part at last.

  1894

III

COMRADES

(Read at the Sixtieth Annual Convention of the Psi Upsilon Fraternity at Dartmouth College, Hanover, N. H., May 18, 1893)

AGAIN among the hills!
The shaggy hills!
The clear arousing air comes like a call
Of bugle notes across the pines, and thrills
My heart as if a hero had just spoken.
Again among the hills!
The jubilant unbroken
Long dreaming of the hills!
Far off, Ascutney smiles as one at peace;
And over all
The golden sunlight pours and fills
The hollow of the earth, like a God's joy.
Again among the hills!
The tranquil hills
That took me as a boy
And filled my spirit with the silences!

O indolent, far-reaching hills, that lie
Secure in your own strength, and take your ease
Like careless giants 'neath the summer sky —
What is it to you, O hills,
That anxious men should take thought for the morrow?
What has your might to do with thought or sorrow
Or cark and cumber of conflicting wills?

47

Lone Pine, that thron'st thyself upon the height,
Aloof and kingly, overlooking all,
Yet uncompanioned, with the Day and Night
For pageant and the winds for festival!
I was thy minion once, and now renew
Mine ancient fealty —
To that which shaped me still remaining true,
And through allegiance only growing free.

So with no foreign nor oblivious heart,
Dartmouth, I seek once more thy granite seat;
Nor only of thy hills I feel me part,
But each encounter of the village street,
The ball-players on the campus, and their shouting,
The runners lithe and fleet,
The noisy groups of idlers, and the songs,
The laughter and the flouting —
Spectacled comic unrelated beings
With book in hand,
Who 'mid all stir of life, all whirl of rhythms,
All strivings, lovings, kissings, dreamings, seeings,
Still live apart in some strange land
Of aorists and ohms and logarithms —
All these are mine; I greet them with a shout.
Whether they will or no, they greet me too.
Grave teachers and the students' jocund rout,
Class-room and tennis court, alike they knew
My step once, and they cannot shut me out.

But dearer than the silence of the hills,
And greater than the wisdom of the years,
Is man to man, indifferent of ills,
Triumphant over fears,
To meet the world with loyal hearts that need
No witness of their friendship but the deed.
Such comrades they, the gallant Musketeers,
Wrought by the master-workman of Romance,
Who foiled the crafty Cardinal and saved
A Queen, for episode, — who braved
The utmost malice of mischance,
The utmost enmity of human foes,
But still rode on across the fields of France,
Reckless of knocks and blows,
Careless of sins or woes,
Incurious of each other's hearts, but sure
That each for each would vanquish or endure.

Praise be to you, O hills, that you can breathe
Into our souls the secret of your power !
He is no child of yours, he never knew
Your spirit — were he born beneath
Your highest crags — who bears not every hour
The might, the calm of you
About him, that sublime
Unconsciousness of all things great, —
Built on himself to stand the shocks of Time
And scarred not shaken by the bolts of Fate.

And praise to thee, my college, that the lore
Of ages may be pondered at thy feet!
That for thy sons each sage and seer of yore
His runes may still repeat!
Praise that thou givest to us understanding
To wring from the world's heart
New answers to new doubts — to make the landing
On shores that have no chart!
Praise for the glory of knowing,
And greater glory of the power to know!
Praise for the faith that doubts would overthrow,
And which through doubts to larger faith is growing!
The sons of science are a wrangling throng,
Yet through their labor what the sons of song
Have wrought in clay, at last
In the bronze is cast,
And wind and rain no more can work it wrong.

But more than strength and more than truth
Oh praise the love of man and man!
Praise it for pledge of our eternal youth!
Praise it for pulse of that great gush that ran
Through all the worlds, when He
Who made them clapped his hands for glee,
And laughed Love down the cycles of the stars.
Praise all that plants it in the hearts of men,
All that protects it from the hoof that mars,

The weed that stifles; praise the rain
That rains upon it and the sun that shines,
Till it stretch skyward with its laden vines!

Praise, then, for thee, Psi Upsilon!
And never shame if it be said
Thou carest little for the head,
All for the heart; for this is thy desire.
Not for the social grace thou mayst impart,
Not for the love of letters or of art,
Albeit thou lovest them, burns thy sacred fire.
Not to add one more whip to those that drive
Men onward in the struggle to survive,
Not to spur weary brain and tired eyes on
To toil for prizes, not, Psi Upsilon,
To be an annex to collegiate chairs
Or make their lapses good!
Make thou no claim of use
For poor excuse
Why thou shouldst climb thy holier stairs
Toward ends by plodders dimly understood.
No, for the love of comrades only, thou!
The college is the head and thou the heart.
Keep thou thy nobler part,
And wear the Bacchic ivy on thy brow.

+   *Comrades, pour the wine to-night,*
      For the parting is with dawn.

Oh, the clink of cups together,
  With the daylight coming on!
    Greet the morn
    With a double horn,
When strong men drink together!

Comrades, gird your swords to-night,
  For the battle is with dawn.
Oh, the clash of shields together,
  With the triumph coming on!
    Greet the foe
    And lay him low,
When strong men fight together.

Comrades, watch the tides to-night,
  For the sailing is with dawn.
Oh, to face the spray together,
  With the tempest coming on!
    Greet the Sea
    With a shout of glee,
When strong men roam together.

Comrades, give a cheer to-night,
  For the dying is with dawn.
Oh, to meet the stars together,
  With the silence coming on!
    Greet the end
    As a friend a friend,
When strong men die together.

       — Hark, afar
The **rising of** the wind **among the pines,**
The runic wind, full **of old legendries !**
It talks to the ancient trees
Of sights and signs .
And strange earth-creatures strong to make or **mar,** —
Such tales **as** when the firelight flickered out
In the old days men **heard** and had no doubt.
O wind, what is your spell?
Borne on your cry, the ages slip **away,**
And **lo,** I **too am of** that elder day;
I crouch **by the logs and hear**
With credent ear
And simple marvel **the far** tales men tell.

There came three women to a youth, and one
Was brown and old, and like the bark of trees
Her wrinkled skin was rough to look upon;
And one was tall and stately, and her brow
Broad with large thought and many masteries,
Yet bent a little as who saith "I trow;"
The third was like a breath of morning blown
Across the hills in May, so blithe, **so** fair,
With brave blue eyes, and on her yellow hair
A glory by the yellow sunlight thrown.

  And the youth's heart flamed as a crackling fire,
  For *his eyes were full of his heart's desire.*

And the old crone said to him, " Come,
For I will give thee Power."
And the tall dame said to him, " Come,
I will give thee Wisdom and Craft."
And the maid of the morning said to him, " Come,
And I will give thee Love."

And the youth was still as a burnt-out fire,
For he knew not which was his heart's desire.

Then spake the maid again ;
" Oh, folly of men !
What thing is this whereat he starts and muses?
Not twice the Dames of Birth
Bring gifts for mirth.
Choose, if thou wilt ; but he that chooses, loses."

. . . Night on the hills !
And the ancient stars emerge.
The silence of their mighty distances
Compels the world to peace.   Now sinks the surge
Of life to a soft stir of mountain rills,
And over the swarm and urge
Of eager men sleep falls and darkling ease.

Night on the hills !
Dark mother-Night, draw near ;
Lay hands on us and whisper words of cheer
So softly, oh, so softly !   Now may we

Be each **as** one that leaves his midnight task
And throws his casement open ; and **the air**
Comes up across the lowlands from the **Sea**
And cools his temples, as a maid might **ask**
With **shy caress what** speech would never **dare ;**
And he leans back to her demure desires,
And as a dream sees far below
The city with its lights aglow
And blesses in his heart his **brothers** there;
Then toward the eternal stars **again** aspires.

1893

ONE LEAF MORE

*(**Read at the** Dinner given by the Psi Upsilon Association of
Washington, February **7,** 1893. to Joseph R. Hawley, on
the occasion of his re-election to the United States Senate)*

Sir, I would do you honor in some way
   If my poor hand could lay a laurel more
On brows already thick with martial **bay**
   And ivy evergreen, the scholar's store,
And civic oak new-garlanded to-day
   To bind afresh where oft were bound before
Its fronds forensic and are bound for aye.

But you need not a poet's voice to tell
   The people who have honored you so long

Why they should love you whom they know so well.
  Still less does any here require my song
That he should praise you whom our hearts impel
  To hail with homage, heartfelt, deep, and strong,
To which my speech is but a tinkling bell.

Still let me praise you, though more fame accrue
  To me than you by praising.   Praise is more
For him that gives than him to whom 't is due.
  He that receives it has a bounteous store
And needs it not.   Who gives, grows just and true
  By speaking justly.   You are as before,
But we are better that we honor you.
  1893

SPRING

*(Read at the Sixty-third Annual Convention of the Psi Upsilon
    Fraternity at the University of Michigan, Ann Arbor, Mich.,
    May 7, 1896)*

I SAID in my heart, " I am sick of four walls and a
    ceiling.
I have need of the sky.
I have business with the grass.
I will up and get me away where the hawk is wheeling,
Lone and high,
And the slow clouds go by.
I will get me away to the waters that glass
The clouds as they pass,

56

To the waters that lie
Like the **heart of a maiden aware of a doom drawing**
    nigh
And dumb for **sorcery of impending joy.**
I will get me **away to** the woods.
Spring, like a huntsman's boy,
Halloos along the hillsides and unhoods
The falcon in my will.
The dogwood calls me, **and the sudden** thrill
That breaks **in** apple blooms down country roads
Plucks me by the sleeve and nudges **me away.**
The sap is in the boles to-day,
And in my veins **a** pulse that yearns and goads."

When **I got to the** woods, I found out
What the Spring was about,
With her **gypsy** ways
And her heart ablaze,
Coming up from the south
With the wander-lure **of witch songs in her** mouth.
For the sky
Stirred and grew **soft and swimming as a lover's eye**
As she went by ;
The **air**
Made love to all it **touched, as if** its care
Were all to spare ;
The earth
Prickled with lust of birth;

The woodland streams
Babbled the incoherence of the thousand dreams
Wherewith the warm sun teems.
And out of the frieze
Of the chestnut trees
I heard
The sky and the fields and the thicket find voice in a
    bird.
The goldenwing — hark !
How he drives his song
Like a golden nail
Through the hush of the air !
I thrill to his cry in the leafage there;
I respond to the new life mounting under the bark.
I shall not be long
To follow
With eft and bulrush, bee and bud and swallow,
On the old trail.

Spring in the world !
And all things are made new !
There was never a mote that whirled
In the nebular morn,
There was never a brook that purled
When the hills were born,
There was never a leaf uncurled —
Not the first that grew —
Nor a bee-flight hurled,

Nor a bird-note skirled,
Nor a cloud-wisp swirled
In the depth of the blue,
More alive and afresh and impromptu, more thought-
	less and certain and free,
More a-shout with the glee
Of the Unknown new-burst on the wonder, than here,
	than here,
In the re-wrought sphere
Of the new-born year —
Now, now,
When the greenlet sings on the red-bud bough
Where the blossoms are whispering " I and thou," —
" I and thou,"
And a lass at the turn looks after her lad with a dawn
	on her brow,
And the world is just made — now !

Spring in the heart !
With her pinks and pearls and yellows !
Spring, fellows,
And we too feel the little green leaves a-start
Across the bare-twigged winter of the mart.
The campus is reborn in us to-day;
The old grip stirs our hearts with new-old joy;
Again bursts bonds for madcap holiday
The eternal boy.

For we have not come here for long debate
Nor taking counsel for our household order,
Howe'er we make a feint of serious things, —
For all the world as in affairs of state
A word goes out for war along the border
To further or defeat the loves of kings.
We put our house to rights from year to year,
But that is not the call that brings us here ;
We have come here to be glad.

Give a rouse, then, in the Maytime
  For a life that knows no fear !
Turn night-time into daytime
  With the sunlight of good cheer !
    For it's always fair weather
    When good fellows get together
With a stein on the table and a good song ringing
  clear.

When the wind comes up from Cuba
  And the birds are on the wing,
And our hearts are patting juba
  To the banjo of the spring,
    Then there 's no wonder whether
    The boys will get together,
With a stein on the table and a cheer for everything.

For we 're all frank-and-twenty
  When the spring is in the air,

And we've faith and hope a-plenty,
  *And we've life and love **to spare**;*
    And it's birds of a feather
    When we all get together,
*With a stein on the table **and a heart without a care**.*

For we know the world is glorious
  And the goal a golden thing,
And that God is not censorious
  When his children have their fling;
    And life slips its tether
    When the boys get together,
With a stein on the table in the fellowship of spring. ✛

A road runs east and a road runs west
From the table where we sing ;
And the lure of the one is a roving quest,
And the lure of the other a lotus dream.
And the eastward road leads into the West
Of the lifelong chase of the vanishing gleam ;
And the westward road leads into **the** East,
Where the spirit from striving is released,
Where the soul like a child in God's arms lies
And forgets the lure of the butterflies.
And west is east, if you follow the trail to the end ;
And east is west, if you follow the trail to the end ;
And the East and the West in the spring of **the**
    world shall blend
As a man and a woman that plight

Their troth in the warm spring night.
And the spring for the East is the sap in the heart of
a tree;
And the spring for the West is the will in the wings
of a bird;
But the spring for the East and the West alike shall be
An urge in their bones and an ache in their spirit, a
word
That shall knit them in one for Time's foison, once
they have heard.

And do I not hear
The first low stirring of that greater spring
Thrill in the underworld of the cosmic year?
The wafture of scant violets presaging
The roses and the tasselled corn to be;
A yearning in the roots of grass and tree;
A swallow in the eaves;
The hint of coming leaves;
The signals of the summer coming up from Arcadie!

For surely in the blind deep-buried roots
Of all men's souls to-day
A secret quiver shoots.
An underground compulsion of new birth
Lays hold upon the dark core of our being,
And unborn blossoms urge their uncomprehended way
Toward the outer day.
Unconscious, dumb, unseeing,

darkness in **us is aware**
omething potent **burning through the earth,**
omething **vital in the procreant air.**

a spring, indeed?
do we stir and mutter in **our dreams,**
y to sleep again?
at warrant have we that **we give not heed**
the caprices of an idle **brain**
t in its slumber deems
world of slumber real **as it seems?**
—
ing's not to be mistaken.
en her first far flute notes blow
Across the snow,
Bird, beast, and blossom know
That **she is there.**
The very bats awaken
That hang in clusters **in Kentucky caves**
All winter, breathless, motionless, asleep,
And feel no alteration of the air,
For all year long those vasty caverns keep,
Winter and summer, even temperature;
And yet when April whistles on the hill,
Somehow, **far** in those subterranean **naves,**
They know, they **hear her, they** obey her will,
And wake and circle through the vaulted aisles
To find her in the open where she smiles.

So we are somehow sure,
By this dumb turmoil in the soul of man,
Of an impending something.   When the stress
Climbs to fruition, we can only guess
What many-seeded harvest we shall scan;
But from one impulse, like a northering sun,
The innumerable outburst is begun,
And in that common sunlight all men know
A common ecstasy
And feel themselves at one.
The comradeship of joy and mystery
Thrills us more vitally as we arouse,
And we shall find our new day intimate
Beyond the guess of any long ago.
Doubting or elate,
With agony or triumph on our brows,
We shall not fail to be
Better comrades than before ;
For no new sense puts forth in us but we
Enter our fellows' lives thereby the more.

And three great spirits with the spirit of man
Go forth to do his bidding.   One is free,
And one is shackled, and the third, unbound,
Halts yet a little with a broken chain
Of antique workmanship, not wholly loosed,
That dangles and impedes his forthright way.
Unfettered, swift, hawk-eyed, implacable,

The wonder-worker, Science, with his wand,
Subdues an alien world to man's desires.
And Art with wide imaginative wings
Stands by, alert for flight, to bear his lord
Into the strange heart of that alien world
Till he shall live in it as in himself
And know its longing as he knows his own.
Behind a little, where the shadows fall,
Lingers Religion with deep-brooding eyes,
Serene, impenetrable, transpicuous
As the all-clear and all-mysterious sky,
Biding her time to fuse into one act
Those other twain, man's right hand and his left.

For all the bonds shall be broken and rent in sunder,
And the soul of man go free
Forth with those three
Into the lands of wonder ;
Like some undaunted youth,
Afield in quest of truth,
Rejoicing in the road he journeys on
As much as in the hope of journey done.
And the road runs east, and the road runs west,
That his vagrant feet explore ;
And he knows no haste and he knows no rest,
And every mile has a stranger zest
Than the miles he trod before ;
And his heart leaps high in the nascent year

When he sees the purple buds appear;
For he knows, though the great black frost may blight
The hope of May in a single night,
That the spring, though it shrink back under the bark,
But bides its time somewhere in the dark —
Though it come not now to its blossoming,
By the thrill in his heart he knows the spring;
And the promise it makes perchance too soon,
It shall keep with its roses yet in June;
For the ages fret not over a day,
And the greater to-morrow is on its way.

   1896

MEN OF DARTMOUTH

MEN of Dartmouth, give a rouse
For the college on the hill!
For the Lone Pine above her
And the loyal men who love her, —
Give a rouse, give a rouse, with a will!
   For the sons of old Dartmouth,
   The sturdy sons of Dartmouth —
   Though round the girdled earth they roam,
   Her spell on them remains;
   They have the still North in their hearts,
   The hill-winds in their veins,
   And the granite of New Hampshire
   In their muscles and their brains.

They were mighty men of old
That she nurtured at her side,
Till like Vikings they went forth
From the lone and silent North, —
And they strove, and they wrought, and they died.
   But — the sons of old Dartmouth,
   The laurelled sons of Dartmouth —
   The mother keeps them in her heart
   And guards their altar-flame;
   The still North remembers them,
   The hill-winds know their name,
   And the granite of New Hampshire
   Keeps the record of their fame.

Men of **Dartmouth, set** a watch
Lest the old traditions fail!
Stand as brother stands by brother!
Dare a deed for the old Mother!
Greet the world, from **the hills, with a hail!**
   For the sons of old Dartmouth,
   The loyal sons of Dartmouth —
   Around the world they keep for **her**
   Their old **chivalric** faith;
   They have the still North in **their souls,**
   The hill-winds **in** their breath;
   And the granite of New Hampshire
   Is made part of them **till death.**

1894

THE OLD PINE

(*Dartmouth College.*)

IT stood upon the hill like some old chief,
And held communion with the cryptic wind,
Keeping like some dim, unforgotten grief,
The memory of tribesmen autumn-skinned,
Silent and slow as clouds, whose footing passed
Down the remote trails of oblivion
Long since into the shadows of the Past.
Alone, aloof, strong fellow of the sun,
We chose it for our standard in its prime ;
Nor, though no longer grimly from its hill
It fronts the world like Webster, wind nor time
Have felled its austere ghost.   We see it still,
   In alien lands, resurgent and undying,
    Flag of our hearts, from sudden ramparts flying.

1895

IN MEMORIAM

(*A. H. Quint*)

MOURN we who honored him but knew him not ;
   Grieve ye who loved him, looking on his face ;
   Be mindful, Dartmouth, of each strenuous trace
That keeps his loyal record unforgot.

There is no faithlessness in grief, God wot;
　　However high the hope or clear the gaze,
　　There must be tears at every burial-place,
　　Though through the tears the very sky be shot.
For death is like the passing of a star
　　That melts into the splendor of the dawn.
　　Were we beyond this air that blurs our sight
In the clear ether where the angels are,
　　We should behold it still; but now, withdrawn
　　In sunrise, lose it, looking on the light.

1896

DARTMOUTH ODE

I

Out of the hills came a voice to me,
Out of the pine woods a cry:

" THOU hast numbered and named us, O man.　Hast
　　thou *known* us at all?
　Thou hast riven our rocks for their secrets, and
　　measured our heights
As a hillock is measured.　But are we revealed?
　　Canst thou call
　Ascutney thy fellow?　Or is it thou Kearsarge
　　invites?

69

What speech have we given thee, measurer — cleaver
    of stones ?
  For we talk to the day-star at dawning, the night-
    winds o' nights,
And our days are a tongue that thou hearest not,
    digger of bones !

" O you who would know us, come out from the roofs
    you have made,
  And plunge in our waters and breathe the sharp joy
    of the air !
Let the hot sun beat down on your foreheads, lie
    prone in the shade,
  With your hearts to the roots and the mosses, climb
    till you stare
From the summit that juts like an island up into the
    sky !
  Watch the clouds pass by day, and by night let the
    power of Altair
And Arcturus and Vega be on you to lift you on high !

" For our heart is not down on the maps, nor our
    magic in books ;
  But the lover that seeks us shall find us, and keep
    in his heart
Every rune of our slow-heaving hillsides, the spaces
    and nooks
  Of our woodlands, the sleep of our waters. His
    thoughts shall be part

Of our thoughts, and his ways shall be with us. His
    spirit shall flee
  From the gluttons of fact. He shall dwell, as the
    hills dwell, apart.
He only that loves us and lives with us, knows what
    we be."

I hear you, O woods and hills !
I hearken, O wind of the North !

II

Daughter of the woods and hills, Dartmouth, my stern
Rock-boned and wind-brown sibyl of the snows!
First in thy praise whom we can never praise
Enough, I lay my laurel in my turn
Before thee in thy uplands. No one goes
Forth from thy granite through the summer days,
And many a land of apple and of rose,
Keeping in his heart more faithfully than I
The love of thy grim hills and northern sky.

Mother of Webster ! Mother of men ! Being great,
Be greater ; let the honor of thy past,
For which we sit in festival, elate,
Be but the portent of thy larger fate,
The adumbration of a deed more vast.
With eyes upon the future, thou and we

Shall better celebrate the past we praise,
And in the pledge of unaccomplished days
Find a new joy thrill through our pride in thee.

III

O Dartmouth, nurse of men, I see your games
To make men strong, your books to make them wise;
But there is other sight than that of eyes,
And other strength than that which strikes and maims.
What hast thou done to purge the passions pure,
To wake the myriad instincts that lie sleeping
Within us unaroused and undivined,
As forests in a hazel-nut endure ;
To fashion finelier our joy and weeping,
Inspire us intuitions swift and sure,
And give us soul as manifold as mind;
To make us scholars in the lore of feeling,
And turn the world to beauty and revealing ?

O justly proud of thy first strenuous years !
Be not content that thou hast nurtured well
The hardy prowess of thy pioneers.
Among thy fellows bold, be thou the first,
Still guarding sacredly the antique well,
To seek new springs to quench the ages' thirst.
Take up the axe, O woodman of the soul,
And break new paths through tangled ignorance ;
Dare the unknown, till on thy jubilant glance

The prairies of the spirit shall unroll.
For thou mayest teach us all that thou hast taught,
Nor slay the earlier instinct of the Faun,
Whose intimacy with earth and air withdrawn,
There rests but hearsay knowledge in our thought.
And thou mayest make us the familiars of
The woodlands of desire, the crags of fate,
The lakes of worship and the dells of love,
Even as the Faun is Nature's intimate.
For God lacks not his seers, and Art is strong,
And spirit unto spirit utters speech,
Nor is there any heaven beyond the reach
Of them that know the masteries of Song.

IV

Oh, the mind and its kingdoms are goodly, and well
    for the brain
  That has craft to discover and cunning to bind to
    its will
And wisdom to weigh at its worth all the wealth they
    contain.
  But the heart has its empire as well, and he shall
    fare ill
Who has learned not the way to its meadows. His
    knowledge shall be
  A bitter taste in his heart; he shall spit at his skill;
And the days of his life shall be sterile and salt as the
    sea.

Ay, save the man's love be made greater, even know-
    ledge shall wane,
  And burn to the mere dry shrivelled mummy of
    thought,
As the sweet grass withers and dies if it get not the
    rain.
  But we — oh, what have we done that the heart
    should be taught?
We have given men brawn — without love 't is the
    Brute come again;
  We have given men brain — without love 't is the
    Fiend. Is there aught
We have given to greaten the soul, we who dare to
    shape men?

Oh, train we the body for beauty, and train we the soul
  Not only as mind but as man, not to know but to be!
Give us masters to fashion our hearts! Let the fool
    be a mole
  And burrow his life out; the wise man shall be as
    a tree
That sends down his roots to the mole-world, but
    laughs in the air
  With his flowers, and his branches shall stretch to
    the sun to get free;
And the shepherds and husbandmen feed of the fruit
    he shall bear.

  125th anniversary of the college, 1894

A WINTER THOUGHT OF DARTMOUTH
IN MANHATTAN

OLD Mother!
Mother off in the hills, by the banks of the beautiful
river!
— River lacquered with pale green luminous ice
Now, and the shouldered ridges ermined with flushed
white snow —
Our thoughts go back to thee, Mother,
Straggle up the Connecticut, and by Bellows Falls
and the Junction,
ind thee at last on thy hills, and embrace thy knees,
old Mother.

do not follow our thoughts upon that journey;
have left thee, as men leave mothers,
osing and wedding their wives and cleaving
thenceforth to them only.

he is stronger than thou, she who now holds us;
iat sits by the sea, new-crowned with a five-fold
ara;
the great twin harbors, our lady of rivers and
ands;
topped Manhattan,
et reeded round with the masts of the five
at oceans

75

Flowering the flags of all nations, flaunting and
    furling, —
City of ironways, city of ferries,
Sea-Queen and Earth-Queen!

Look, how the line of her roofs coming down from the
    north
Breaks into surf-leap of granite — jagged sierras —
Upheaval volcanic, lined sharp on the violet sky
Where the red moon, lop-sided, past the full,
Over their ridge swims in the tide of space,
And the harbor waves laugh softly, silently.

Look, how the overhead train at the Morningside
    curve
Loops like a sea-born dragon its sinuous flight,
Loops in the night in and out, high up in the air,
Like a serpent of stars with the coil and undulant
    reach of waves.

From under the Bridge at noon
See from the yonder shore how the great curves rise
    and converge,
Like the beams of the universe, like the masonry of
    the sky,
Like the arches set for the corners of the world,
The foundation-stone of the orbic spheres and spaces.

Is she not fair and terrible, O Mother —
City of Titan thews, deep-breasted, colossal-limbed,
Splendid with the spoil of nations, myriad-mooded
Manhattan?
Behold, we are hers — she has claimed us ; and who
has power to withstand her?

Nevertheless, old Mother, we do not forget thee.
Thine is the past!
Thine are the old recollections, the love of the boy-
hood still in us,
As the sprout still lives in the bough and remembers
March in the summer.
Sword and ploughshare and engine forget not the days
When the crude ore went to the smelting and the
hammers rang on thy anvils.

This is a letter we send from ocean-dominioned
Manhattan,
Bearing the love of a boy from the heart of a man,
Bearing the never-evading remembrance of thee and
the hills and the river,
Thornton and Wentworth and Reed and the century-
hollowed stairways of Dartmouth,
The old rooms where we laughed and strove and sang,
Where others now — hark, do I hear them? —
Sing in the winter night, while Orion rises and glistens.

For the Dartmouth Dinner, New York, 1898.

OUR LIEGE LADY, DARTMOUTH

Up with the green! Comrades, our Queen
Over the hill-tops comes to convene
   Liege men all to her muster.
Easy her chain! Blithe be her reign,
Queened in our heart's love, never a stain
   Dimming her 'scutcheon's lustre!
Up with the green! God save our Queen!
Throned on the hills of her highland demense,
Royal and beautiful, wise and serene,
    Our Liege Lady, Dartmouth!

Gallant and leal! Truer than steel!
Loyally gather about her and kneel
   Here at her flag's unfurling.
Welcome her near cheer upon cheer,
Shout till the hawk far above us may hear,
   Where the clouds in the sky are curling.
Starry her fame, Heaven-born dame!
Cannon and trumpet salute her high name!
Hear the ranks ring with the royal acclaim:
    Our Liege Lady, Dartmouth!

Laurel and vine, what shall we twine
Meet for her brow who sits under the pine
   Far from the mad town's jarring?
Gracious and fair, see in her hair

Jewels her noblest have brought her to wear,
    Won in the world's stern warring!
Stainless her throne! Royal and lone!
Born in the purple the sunsets have thrown
Over the mountains by God's grace her own,
        Our Liege Lady, Dartmouth!

Hail to the Queen! Look, where the green
Folds of her banners about her are seen,
    Flash of her knight's cuirasses!
True-hearted throng, break into song!
Rally her cavaliers, faithful and strong!
    Shout as her ensign passes:
Up with the green! God save our Queen!
Throned on the hills of her highland demesne,
Royal and beautiful, wise and serene,
        Our Liege Lady, Dartmouth!

1891

HANOVER WINTER-SONG

see Dante Lyric

Ho, a song by the fire!
(Pass the pipes, fill the bowl!)
Ho, a song by the fire!
— With a skoal! . . .
For the wolf wind is whining in the doorways,
And the snow drifts deep along the road,
And the ice-gnomes are marching from their Norways,

79

And the great white cold walks abroad.
(Boo-oo-o ! pass the bowl !)
    For here by the fire
    We defy frost and storm.
    Ha, ha ! we are warm
    And we have our hearts' desire;
    For here 's four good fellows
    And the beechwood and the bellows,
    And the cup is at the lip
    In the pledge of fellowship.
        Skoal !

For " Dartmouth Songs," 1898.

IV

THE FAUN

(A Fantasy of the Washington Woodlands.)

I WILL go out to grass with that old King,
For I am weary of clothes and cooks.
I long to paddle with the throats of brooks,
To lie down with the clover
Tickling me all over,
And watch the boughs above me sway and swing.
Come, I will pluck off custom's livery,
Nor longer be a lackey to old Time.
Time shall serve me, and at my feet shall fling
The spoil of listless minutes.   I shall climb
The wild trees for my food, and run
Through dale and upland as a fox runs free,
Laugh for cool joy and sleep i' the warm sun, —
And men will call me mad, like that old King.

For I am woodland-natur'd, and have made
Dryads my bedfellows,
And I have played
With the sleek Naiads in the splash of pools
And made a mock of gowned and trousered fools.
And I am half Faun now, and my heart goes
Out to the forest and the crack of twigs,
The drip of wet leaves, and the low soft laughter
Of brooks that chuckle o'er old mossy jests
And say them over to themselves, the nests

83

Of squirrels, and the holes the chipmunk digs,
Where through the branches the slant rays
Dapple with sunlight the leaf-matted ground,
And th' wind comes with blown vesture rustling after,
And through the woven lattice of crisp sound
A bird's song lightens like a maiden's face.

O wildwood Helen, let them strive and fret,
Those goggled men with their dissecting knives!
Let them in charnel-houses pass their lives
And seek in death life's secret!   And let
Those hard-faced worldlings, prematurely old,
Gnaw their thin lips with vain desire to get
Portia's fair fame or Lesbia's carcanet,
Or crown of Cæsar or Catullus,
Apicius' lampreys or Crassus' gold!
For these consider many things — but yet
By land nor sea
They shall not find the way to Arcadie,
The old home of the awful heart-dear Mother,
Whereto child-dreams and long rememberings lull us,
Far from the cares that overlay and smother
The memories of old woodland outdoor mirth
In the dim first life-burst centuries ago,
The sense of the freedom and nearness of Earth —
Nay, this they shall not know;
For who goes thither
Leaves all the cark and clutch of his soul behind,

The doves defiled and the serpents shrined,
The hates that wax and the hopes that wither;
Nor does he journey, seeking where it be,
But wakes and finds himself in Arcadie.

Hist! there's a stir in the brush.
Was it a face through the leaves?
Back of the laurels a scurry and rush
Hillward, then silence, except for the thrush
That throws one song from the dark of the bush
And is gone; and I plunge in the wood, and the swift
    soul cleaves
Through the swirl and the flow of the leaves, .
As a swimmer stands with his white limbs bare to the
    sun
For the space that a breath is held, and drops in the
    sea;
And the undulant woodland folds round me, intimate,
    fluctuant, free,
Like the clasp and the cling of waters, and the reach
    and the effort is done; —
There is only the glory of living, exultant to be.

Oh, goodly damp smell of the ground!
Oh, rough sweet bark of the trees!
Oh, clear sharp cracklings of sound!
Oh, life that's a-thrill and a-bound
With the vigor of boyhood and morning and the
    noontide's rapture of ease!

Was there ever a weary heart in the world?
A lag in the body's urge, or a flag of the spirit's
    wings?
Did a man's heart ever break
For a lost hope's sake?
For here there is lilt in the quiet and calm in the
    quiver of things.
Ay, this old oak, grey-grown and knurled,
Solemn and sturdy and big,
Is as young of heart, as alert and elate in his rest,
As the oriole there that clings to the tip of the twig
And scolds at the wind that it buffets too rudely his
    nest.

Hear! hear! hear!
Listen! the word
Of the mocking-bird!
Hear! hear! hear!
I will make all clear;
I will let you know
Where the footfalls go
That through the thicket and over the hill
Allure, allure.
How the bird-voice cleaves
Through the weft of leaves
With a leap and a thrill
Like the flash of the weaver's shuttle, swift and
    sudden and sure!

And lo, he is gone — even while I turn
The wisdom of his runes to learn.
He knows the mystery of the wood,
The secret of the solitude ;
But he will not tell, he will not tell
— For all he promises so well.

Oh, what is it breathes in the air ?
Oh, what is it touches my cheek ?
There's a sense of a presence that lurks in the
    branches.   But where ?
Is it far, is it far to seek ?

Brother, lost brother !
Thou of mine ancient kin !
Thou of the swift will that no ponderings smother !
The dumb life in me fumbles out to the shade
Thou lurkest in.
In vain — evasive ever through the glade
Departing footsteps fail ;
And only where the grasses have been pressed
Or by snapt twigs I follow a fruitless trail.
So — give o'er the quest !
Sprawl on the roots and moss !
Let the lithe garter squirm across my throat !
Let the slow clouds and leaves above me float
Into mine eyeballs and across, —
Nor think them further ! Lo, the marvel ! now,
Thou whom my soul desireth, even thou

Sprawl'st by my side, who fled'st at my pursuit.
I hear thy fluting ; at my shoulder there
I see the sharp ears through the tangled hair,
And birds and bunnies at thy music mute.

Cool ! cool ! cool !
Cool and sweet
The feel of the moss at my feet !
And sweet and cool
The touch of the wind, of the wind !

Cool wind out of the blue,
At the touch of you
A little wave crinkles and flows
All over me down to my toes.

" Coo-loo ! Coo-loo !"
Hear the doves in the tree tops croon *
" Coo-loo ! Coo-loo !"
Love comes soon.

" June ! June !"
The veery sings,
Sings and sings,
" June ! June !"
A pretty tune !

Wind with your weight of perfume,
Bring me the bluebells' bloom !

88

Ah, too much charmed I seek thee, and again
Thou meltest in the shadows.   Now the breath
Of evening comes, and at the word she saith
I rise and turn back toward the streets of men.
First up the hill to where the trees are few,
To pause halfway between the wood and town
And, strengthened with the Faun's delight, look
    down
Upon the roofs I am returning to.

The fervid breath of our flushed Southern May
Is sweet upon the city's throat and lips,
As a lover's whose tired arm slips
Listlessly over the shoulder of a queen.
Far away
The river melts in the unseen.
Oh, beautiful Girl-City, how she dips
Her feet in the stream
With a touch that is half a kiss and half a dream!
Her face is very fair,
With flowers for smiles and sunlight in her hair.

My westland flower-town, how serene she is!
Here on this hill from which I look at her,
All is still as if a worshipper
Left at some shrine his offering.
Soft winds kiss
My cheek with a slow lingering.

A luring whisper where the laurels stir
Wiles my heart back to woodland-ward again.
But lo,
Across the sky the sunset couriers run,
And I remain
To watch the imperial pageant of the sun
Mock me, an impotent Cortez here below,
With splendors of its vaster Mexico.

O Eldorado of the templed clouds !
O golden city of the western sky !
Not like the Spaniard would I storm thy gates;
Not like the babe stretch chubby hands and cry
To have thee for a toy ; but, far from crowds,
Like my Faun-brother in the ferny glen,
Peer from the wood's edge while thy glory waits,
And in the darkening thickets plunge again.

1894

SWALLOW SONG

(From the Greek)

HURRAH, the swallow, the swallow is come,
Bringing the spring from his southern home,
   The beautiful hours, the beautiful year !
Hurrah, the swallow is back from his flight,
With his back of jet and his breast of white,
   The Summer's earliest harbinger !

Come, roll out some figs from your cellar, old fellow!
Bring a beaker of wine that is ruddy and mellow,
  And a wicker crate heaped up with cheeses!
Be it bread of pulse or bread of wheat,
The swallow will not disdain to eat.
  Oh, the swallow and spring and the buds and the
      breezes!

Will you send us away, or shall we receive
The best that your larder is able to give?
  We warn you — be generous, for if you say nay,
Your gate shall be torn from its hinge and destroyed,
Or your wife, who is sitting within, be decoyed, —
  She is small, we can easily bear her away.

Bring your gifts to the swallow, but if you bring aught,
Bring all that you can, bring more than is sought;
  Open your doors for his welcoming;
For we are not grey old men, not we,
But children who laugh in juvenile glee,
  And sing in life's springtide this song of the spring.

1883

A HEALTH. TO E. C. S.

HERE 's your health in Burgundy
  And here 's your health in rye,
Until our betters drink your health
  In nectar by and bye.

1897

THE DRAMATIST.   TO M. K.

NOT to reveal one mystery
  That lurks beneath life's garment-hem —
Alas, I write of human hearts
  Because I cannot fathom them.

1898

DELSARTE

As at the altar of the unknown God
  Even so we stood before the shrine of Art.
Ignorant, we worshipped — till the hill was trod
  By the Apostle.   Whom but thee, Delsarte?

1893

WORLD AND POET

"SING to us, Poet, for our hearts are broken;
Sing us a song of happy, happy love,
Sing of the joy that words leave all unspoken, —
The lilt and laughter of life, oh sing thereof!
Oh, sing of life, for we are sick and dying;
Oh, sing of joy, for all our joy is dead;
Oh, sing of laughter, for we know but sighing;
Oh, sing of kissing, for we kill instead!"
How should he sing of happy love, I pray,
Who drank love's cup of anguish long ago?
How should he sing of life and joy and day,

Who whispers Death to end his night of woe?
And yet the Poet took his lyre and sang,
Till all the dales with happy echoes rang.

1891

THE SOUTH

AH, where the hot wind with sweet odors laden
Across the roses faintly beats his wings,
Lifting a lure of subtle murmurings
Over the still pools that the herons wade in,
Telling of some far sunset-bowered Aidenn,
And in an orange-tree an oriole sings,
Whereunder lies, dreaming of unknown things,
With orange-blossoms wreathed, a radiant maiden, —
There is the poet's land, there would I lie
Under magnolia blooms and take no care,
And let my eyes grow languid and my mouth
Glow with the kisses of the amorous air,
And breathe with every breath the luxury
Of the hot-cheeked, sweet, heavy-lidded South.

1883

A CAPRICE OF OGAROW. TO M. P.

IT is a sweet coquetting. I can see
Above the fan the rogue eyes' merry leer,
The fitful feigned retreatings that appear
To court pursuit, the cheeks that dimple with glee

Like a lake struck by a light wind, feet that flee
  A little way and wait as if for fear
  Light love should yield the chase, — so sweet and
    clear
  The violin speech tells its tale to me.
O art's rose lady, such themes have their part
  In beryl-wrought rare delicate interludes;
  But give not unto these thy queenlier art.
Rather shouldst thou unsphinx the rarer moods
  Of Chopin passioning in a star's red heart,
  Or Schubert sighing in the solitudes.

1887

THOMAS WILLIAM PARSONS

THE maiden knew the hero was divine, —
For when she saw him, was she not content?
So in the satisfaction of the heart
We find his praise, nor with too noisy art
Proclaim the beauty past all ornament
Of his precise and unsuperfluous line.

  1892

BEETHOVEN'S THIRD SYMPHONY.

PASSION and pain, the outcry of despair,
  The pang of unattainable desire,
  And youth's delight in pleasures that expire,
  And sweet high dreamings of the good and fair

Clashing in swift soul-storm, through which no prayer
  Uplifted stays the destined death-stroke dire!
  Then through a mighty sorrowing as through fire
  The soul burnt pure yearns forth into the air
Of the dear earth and, with the scent of flowers
  And song of birds refreshed, takes heart again,
  Made cheerier with this drinking of God's wine,
And turns with healing to the world of men;
  And high above a sweet strong angel towers
  And Love makes life triumphant and divine.

1888

AUGUST

THE white sky and the white sea run
Their twin pearl-splendors into one,
  Nor can the eye distinguish these,
  Enchanted by the diableries
The mist-witch conjures in the sun.
Landward a white birch, like a nun,
  Whispers her leafy rosaries.
  Beyond, where the still woodland is,
The blue west leadens into dun,
  Close to the dark tops of the trees.

1886

A BALLADE OF MYSTERIES

Doctor, I pray you, do no more wrong
  To the drugged dog there in the horrid room.
Come, unmuzzle ; disclose how the stars prolong
  Thin lines of light through the infinite gloom,
  And how life sprang in the primal spume.
Then I 'll tell you how the bells' ding-dong
  Holds sweet talk with the birds i' the broom,
And the poet's heart is astir with song.

Sage, who discernest in winter's thong
  The thought at the heart of June's perfume,
Say, how grows the weak babe wise and strong,
  And how is Thought born, and by whom
  May the Fates be lured from the pitiless loom,
And what is Right and what is Wrong ?
  Then I 'll tell you why the breakers boom,
And the poet's heart is astir with song.

Priest, tell me now, ere the even-song,
  How God lay hid in the Virgin's womb,
Who filleth the depth and the height of the long
  Sky-reaches, and how men's mouths consume
  His flesh that rose from the sacred tomb.
Then I 'll tell you how the clouds give tongue
  To a message from God of a grand sweet doom,
And the poet's heart is astir with song.

Princess, say how the heart makes room
For love, where the cares of a kingdom throng.
  Then I 'll tell you why the roses bloom
And the poet's heart is astir with song.

  1887

THE SHADOWS

DUMB as the dead, with furtive tread,
  Unseen, unheard, unknown, —
And never a Gloom that turns his head
  As they stride where I crouch alone!

For this is the grisliest horror there
  As the brutal bulks go by ;
Right on they fare, with a stony stare,
  Nor heed me where I lie.

Though I strain my eyes as I freeze and cringe
  Till the sockets sizzle dry,
And the eyeball shrieks like a rusty hinge,
  They will never impinge mine eye.

I shall see nought but the silver darks
  Of the sky and the dim sea,
Where horrid silver loops and arcs
  Foam phosphorent at me.

  7   97

But the cliff, the cliff ! Lo, where thereon
  Their silent shadows file,
One after one, one after one,
  Mile on remorseless mile.

Dull red, like embers in a grate,
  Against the sulphur crag,
They play about the feet of Fate
  Their awful game of tag.

1893

ANGRO-MAINYUS

I AM the Most High God;
Worship thou me !
Put not up vain prayers to avert my wrath,
For my wrath shall fall like the thunderbolt
And thou shalt be cleft asunder as an oak.

I am Angro-mainyus, the Most High God.
Cry not unto me for mercy, for I am merciless.
Sin and Death are my ministers,
And my ways are ways of torture and the shedding
    of blood.
I am the Lord thy God.

I am the Destroyer.
My sword is as fire in the forest;

My feet are inexorable.
Ask me not to deliver thee from evil.
I am Evil.

Ahura-mazda is God too,   .
The beneficent one, the savior!
He dwelleth in the Sun,
But I in the terror of tempests.
There are two thrones, but one God.

The waves of the sea war mightily,
But in the deeps there is calm.
Ahura-mazda and I are one God;
There is war between our legions,
But in us peace.
Behold, he knoweth my thoughts and I his,
And there is no discord in us.

He worketh in light
And I in darkness;
His ways and my ways are asunder.
But blaspheme not, calling me " Devil,"
Neither saying, " There are two Gods;"
I am the Most High God,
And I and Ahura-mazda are one.

   1888

IMMANENCE

Enthroned above the world although he sit,
Still is the world in him and he in it;
   The selfsame power in yonder sunset glows
That kindled in the lords of Holy Writ.

   1893

TRANSCENDENCE

THOUGH one with all that sense or soul can see,
Not prisoned in his own creations he,
   His life is more than stars or winds or angels —
The sun doth not contain him nor the sea.

   1893

VISITATION

WAS it a dream, or did I see him there,
That quiet presence in my easy-chair?
Surely a sacred hush was in the room,
And a dim sense of legends made the gloom
Of unlit tapers and a dying fire
Rich with the grace of wonderland drawn nigher —
And there across the table, who but he?

I cannot think but that he thought of me,
Far off, in some diviner atmosphere,
And, thinking so, — if he did not appear

Indeed, as I half fancied then, and now
Still sometimes dream, so clear the wide calm **brow,**
Shadowed with **a** sweet seriousness, I see
Across the table in my reverie —
Yet, thinking so, his loving thought had power
To make **me** feel his presence like a flower
That sends a heavy odor through the air,
To make me see him, though he **was not there.**

O gentle ghost! I would that I could deem
That I were worthy of that passing dream.
I would that I could think that my poor song
Had reached thee where thou walkest with the throng
Of gracious poets in their glory crowned,
Shakespeare and Burns and Shelley laurel-bound,
And pleased thee but so much as thou shouldst turn
And yield one sigh for those who still must mourn
On this harsh earth, one sigh for him whose line
Were too much graced in that one thought of thine.

1891

IN EXCELSIS

I saw a man alone upon a height,
   With face toward heaven. I asked what did he
     there.
"**For** thirty years I have known the stars; to-night,"
   He said, " I see the angels and despair."

1896

THE VEILED LADY

WHOSO hath seen her brow displayed,
  Keeps silence of its bloom or blight.
She passeth through our streets arrayed
  In weeds that screen her from men's sight.
  None knoweth if in that veil bedight
Lurk loathsome hag or lovesome maid.
Whoso hath seen her brow displayed
  Keeps silence of its bloom or blight.

Men pass her daily undismayed,
  Yet often in the sleepless night
Cry "Grace or Gorgon?" sore afraid;
  But no word comes from any wight.
Whoso hath seen her brow displayed,
  Keeps silence of its bloom or blight.

1888

THE MESSENGER

(*For the Picture by G. P. Watts*)

STRONG angel of the peace of God,
  Not wholly undivined thy mien;
Along the weary path I trod
  Thou hast been with me though unseen.

My hopes have been a mad turmoil,
  A clutch and conflict all my life,
The very craft I loved a toil,
  And love itself a seed of strife.

But sometimes in a sudden hour
  I have been great with Godlike calm,
As if thy tranquil world of power
  Flowed in about me like a psalm.

And peace has fallen on my face,
  And stillness on my struggling breath;
And, living, I have known a space
  The hush and mastery of Death.

Stretch out thy hand upon me, thou
  Who comest as the still night comes!
I have not flinched at buffets; now
  Let Strife go by, with all his drums.

1894

HENRY GEORGE

(*Died October* 29, 1897)

OH, be his death a clarion
To hearten, not dismay!
Fight on!
We have not lost the day. . . .

Ay, if the day be lost, what then?
The cause, the cause endures.
Be men —
The triumph yet is yours,

The triumph every cause has won
That called men to be free!
Fight on,
Indomitable as he —

As he, our captain without stain,
The Bayard of the poor.
Be men!
Flinch no man in this hour.

Remember him that knew no fear,
And craved no diadem.
A cheer!
Be that his requiem.

1897

V

BENZAQUEN: A FRAGMENT

BOOK I

SOUL of the East! Thou strong still angel whose
    great wings,
  Stretched moveless in the air, outspread from
    Himalay
To Sinai and the dreaming Nile! Whose ponderings
  Fill the rich womb of Asia with the sons of day!
Under the shadow of whose brooding thought the
    earth
  Breeds mysteries and devotions! Shalt thou not
    alway,
As in the beginning, bring the lords of life to birth?

For we, whom Michael, the fierce spirit of the West,
  Leads to the storm of Heaven with call of drum and
    fife, —
We are the lords of earth, lords of the endless quest,
  Lords of the violent and immitigable strife,
Lords of the lightnings, lords of iron, lords of the
    Deed;
  But thine, O East, the lords of life and the springs
    of life,
Lords of the void spaces of the soul's extreme need.

Therefore to thee, as when at nightfall o'er the hills
  The shadows creep and overhead the silent stars

Kindle their furtive fires, and all the deep heaven
    fills
  With soundless splendors; then the warder Sleep
    unbars
The gates of dream — even so to thee we come and
    seek
  Peace and the mirrored vision that no tumult
    mars,
The wisdom only Death and Night and Silence speak.

Under the cloudlike sweep of those unmoving pinions
  Wherewith the soul of Asia floats and dreams
    unstirred,
High on the slope of that sheer mount whose peak
    dominions
  The valley of Lake Van, roamed over by the Kurd,
Ali the poet lay, and fever crunched his bones;
  And by him moved with gentle step and soothing
    word
The teacher, Benzaquen, and groaned but stilled his
    groans.

At last the sick man slept; and Benzaquen arose
  And walked along the soaring pathway, where
    beneath
The valley lay o'erpurpled; and across his brows
  The wind laid its long fingers gently till his teeth

Relaxed their clenching and his heart grew calm.
    He sighed,
  As one that wakes from a deep trance and with his
      breath
Drinks life in eagerly, and, " Gentle God," he cried,

" How comely in the morning is thy face; how fair
    Among the valleys is the coming of thy feet !
The air is glad of thee ; yea, as a maid the air
    Trembles and blushes for her lover.   Behold, the
        wheat
Bows down before thee in the sun ; the sesame
    Bends low beneath thy kisses, for thy lips are sweet;
The peaches and pomegranates stir and worship thee.

" How loving is the Lord God and how strong withal !
    The fig-tree putteth forth her fruit in the fair
        weather ;
The clusters of the vine hang purple on the wall :
    But the north wind awakes and the black frost strides
        hither,
And the bare boughs stretch gaunt in prayer against
        their doom.
    The hand of the Lord God is upon them and they
        wither ;
The hand of the Lord God is upon them and they
        bloom.

" Praise him, ye hills; praise him, ye beech-trees of
      Sapan!
Praise him, sun and air and divine reach of blue!
Praise him, ye rivers; praise him, violet waves of Van!
   Praise him, clouds and vapors and dear drench of
      the dew!
Praise him, ye caverns of Mount Ala, ye fountains
      welling
   In the groves of Baghlar; for his tarrying is with
      you, —
Here is the garden of the Lord, and this is his dwelling."

He ceased; his chin fell on his bosom and he wept,
   For sudden longing smote him for the boy that lay
Sick in the cavern, his disciple; and he kept
   Weeping, and willingly he could have turned to pray
The Divine Father of all to hear and save the youth,
   But would not; so his heart grew heavier alway.
But him Sandalphon heard, the angel, and had ruth

And came to him; and like a wind he came whose
      touch
   Rustles the leaves in Baghlar.   Thereon Benzaquen
Lifted his eyes and saw him, in apparel such
   As at Baghdad in the schools among the elder men
The young aspirant wears.   " Master," the angel said,
   " Why weepest thou?"   But he, not knowing him,
      again
Let fall his eyes and spake not, sad, uncomforted.

The angel spake on : " In the **streets of Van men say,**
    And in Kharput, **that** Ali, he who did not fail
In the hour when all rejected thee, and in **the day**
    Of exile left thee **not, thy** comfort, waxeth frail
With fever and, without God, in three days is dead,
    For even thy knowledge, wise hakim, doth not avail."
And Benzaquen made answer unto him and said :

" Is my name heard in Van ?   Or in Kharput doth any
    Remember me ?   How know they if I **come or** go ?"
He paused with nostrils wide for scorn of many and
        many ;
    Then sighed again with " Son, all this thou sayest
        is so.
Why troublest thou me ? "   **And** Sandalphon answered
        sweet :
    " Though I be young, I may **speak** wisdom ; yea,
        although
I be not old, **my** conversation **may be meet.**

" Righteous hast thou been from thy youth ; thy voice
        is heard,
    Morning and evening, praising **God.**   Thou hast
        put down
The atheist in the market-place, and with a word
    Confuted them that doubt ; **the** young men of **the**
        town

111

Heard thee and scorned the scoffers. Shall God,
    then, despise
  Thy pleading, or if thou implore him, shall he
    frown?
Open thy heart to him, beseech him and be wise!"

Then Benzaquen rose up and answered, and his
    speech
  Was wrathful: "Knowest thou so much, and know-
    est not this, —
That therefore was I cast out from among them that
    teach;
  And therefore was my name writ down with words
    that hiss
And sear into my soul, *Accurst;* therefore, re-
    belling,
  I bide alone and know no more my father's kiss;
Therefore the caverns of Mount Ala are my
    dwelling!

"Because I would not speak vain words to the All
    Wise,
  Nor blur discretion, babbling. Shall a man aspire
Before Him who controls the inexorable skies
  To say *This thing is good* or *That thing I desire?*
Who then is he takes counsel with the Almighty?
    Who

Enlargeth knowledge and judgment for the Eternal
  Sire?
Who thinks to change his will, or mould his works
  anew?

"Shall the iron argue with the smith what it would
  be?
 Or shall the wrought iron reason with the iron-
  monger
To whom it would be sold? Though all men cry,
  shall He
 Who shifts not, alter? The old seek safety and
  the younger
Folly; but his remorseless laws are not reversed.
 Shall the fruits ripen ere their season if I hunger?
Or shall the desert give forth water if I thirst?

"Consider the stars, how they obey their times and
  seasons;
 Their rising and their setting has been fixed for aye.
When the recurring heavens shall fail, there may be
  reasons
 To hope that God shall hearken unto them that
  pray. . . .
But thou, if thou hast sought me not for disputation
 Or pride of speech but kindly-hearted, make no
  stay,
But get thee to the city to the habitation

"Of Hafiz the physician; beg of him three grains
    Of that elixir that the great Al-Mamun gave
When we two knew him at Baghdad. There yet
        remains
    This one chance to redeem the sick man from the
        grave;
But save this I know not what hope there be in art."
    Sandalphon answered not; angelic natures crave
The soul's guest-welcome, — in the inhospitable heart

They have no power to enter, and they hold their
        peace.
    Even so Sandalphon; and he bowed his comely
        head
With courtesy celestial, then between the trees
    Departed. Benzaquen looked after as he sped
Down the steep pathway with so light a step it
        seemed
    More like the swallow's flight along the ground
        than tread
Of a man walking. But even as he looked he
        dreamed

Self-elsewhered and lost sight, and when he looked
        once more
    Nought moving saw he save the cony in the rocks
And on the air the silent vulture far a-soar.
    And as the shepherd turns at evening with his
        flocks

Foldward, and with the calm of nightfall in his
    thought
Feels, as he passes in the fields the restful ox,
Sweet kinship; so the teacher, strangely peaceful,
    sought

Again his cave, — and lo! upon a rock-shelf there
    Lay the elixir.   All the place was fraught about
With odor, and upon the sleeping Ali's hair
    The sun fell like a mystic wine of light poured out
In cupfuls.   Benzaquen stood motionless and gazed
    Upon the vial with a wild and wondering doubt,
Silent, uncomprehending, ominous, amazed.

*   *   *   *   *   *   *

1893